The first step in learning to read is a big one: from single letters to whole words. That's a lot to ask of young children. To make the transition to reading as simple and easy as possible, why not use the shortest words possible, at least in the very first books that children read? How short can words be and still make a story? Three letters, two letters, one letter? The Bo books use very short words to tell very simple stories, with characters, action, and humor, to help young children cross the threshold into the world of reading. You can read them for free as e-books or buy the paper books for close to their cost, with any author's profit donated to UNICEF.

BO, GO UP!

Text by Larry Baum
Pictures by Joanna Pasek

Made in the USA
Middletown, DE
20 November 2021

53025629R00018